CHRISTMAS IS CANCELED

A HUMOROUS PARANORMAL COZY MYSTERY

CARLY WINTER

Edited by
DIVAS AT WORK EDITING
Cover by
COVEREDBYMELINDA.COM

WESTWARD PUBLISHING / CARLY FALL, LLC

CHRISTMAS IS CANCELED

Will her favorite time of year bring her joy...
or tears?

When Bernie plans a Christmas party with her friends, she's excited to decorate and enjoys buying all the gifts for a white elephant gift exchange.

Days before the festivities, she comes home to discover all her presents have been stolen. With the help of her ghostly grandmother, Ruby, she's determined to investigate who's responsible for ruining her Christmas party... and why.

But when she discovers the perpetrator, will the Christmas spirit come alive in Bernie, or will Christmas be canceled?

CHAPTER 1

As I STEPPED out of the shower, the off-key voice of my dead grandmother's ghost, Ruby, singing *Holly Jolly Christmas* filtered into the bathroom. I loved everything about Christmas: the food, the decorations, the way my heart felt just a little lighter and kinder than it did the rest of the year. I even loved Christmas carols—except when Ruby sang them. Nails on a chalkboard or a chorus of drunk monkeys would have been preferred.

"Ruby, could you please keep it down?" I yelled as I wrapped my hair in a towel. Just as I cleared the steam from the mirror, she appeared behind me and our gazes met in the reflection. She'd died wearing a purple mumu over her thin frame and her long gray hair pulled back into a ponytail. She was stuck that way for eternity.

In an attempt to appear scary, she raised her hands above her and rolled her eyes into the back of her head. In her best ghostly voice, she said, "I am the Ghost of Christmas Past, and you are a party pooper."

"And you aren't scary."

Ruby furrowed her brow and crossed her arms over her

chest. "Is that the Christmas spirit? Telling someone not to sing Christmas carols? I suppose you put pee in the punch instead of tequila during your holiday parties?"

"Gross," I replied, rubbing lotion on my arms. "You're just a little loud for this early in the morning."

"And you, my dear one, are a grinch." With a wave, she stuck out her tongue and faded away.

When Ruby had died three years ago, she'd left me her house in Sedona, Arizona. I'd spent a lot of summers with her while growing up doing all sorts of things my uptight mother wouldn't allow me to do—watch R-rated movies, eat cookies for breakfast, and stay up all night if I so desired. While my own mother, Ruby's daughter, was conservative and rigid, Ruby was all about fun. The more rules there were to break, the happier she was.

Both thrilled at my new start in life and saddened that Ruby and I had lost touch as I entered adulthood, I'd left my house in Louisiana and moved to Sedona. Soon, I realized working as a yoga instructor wasn't going to pay the electric bill, let alone the mortgage, so I turned the big home into a bed and breakfast. After running it for three years, imagine my surprise when I was hit by lightning and discovered that my house was haunted... by my dead grandmother.

"Let's go, Bernie!" Ruby yelled. "We've got so much to do!"

She wasn't wrong. My to-do list for the Christmas party grew each day as it drew near. I'd spent hours upon hours decorating the house and I still wasn't done. Thankfully, my friend, Darla, was going to bring most of the food. She owned the local diner and loved to cook, so she'd volunteered and I'd gladly accepted since I hated cooking and most recipes I attempted were inedible. I still had to shop for the white elephant gift exchange and stop by the liquor store. Ruby also wanted more lights on the outside of the house, but I wasn't going to take my life in my hands to climb a ladder. My handyman, Henry, who helped me with odd jobs around my home, had agreed to come over this afternoon. The ugly Christmas sweater I'd ordered was also late, so I figured I might have to improvise there.

I opened my closet. An impressive array of 80s movies t-shirts hung in a neat row—everything from the *Breakfast Club* to *Working Girl*. Even though I had been born in the middle of that decade, I had a deep appreciation for the movies of that time. What did one wear for Christmas gift shopping? *National Lampoon's Christmas Vacation*, of course. The best Christmas movie ever made.

For good measure, I also wore my Santa cap, red scarf, and jingle bell earrings. No one could ever accuse me of not having any Christmas spirit.

"Don't you look cute?" Ruby said as I entered the kitchen.

"Thank you."

"Can you turn on the lights in the living room and we can take a quick peek before we go?" Ruby asked. "Just to make sure we don't need to pick up any bulbs."

"Sure."

In her ghostly state, Ruby couldn't move inanimate objects, which led to her bossing me around and me complying most of the time. After plugging everything in, I stepped back and admired my work.

The twenty-piece Christmas village sitting on the erected table behind one of the sofas looked as though it may come alive at any second. Ruby had collected pieces during her life and I'd added a few as well. Figurines of kids running through the snow and adults shopping at the various stores scattered across the town. "I love this thing," Ruby said quietly as she bent over and stared at the shops. "The dog groomer was always my favorite."

I smiled and walked over to join her. "I also like the church and the cookie factory," I said.

3

"You know what it's missing?" she asked, standing upright. "A Santa figurine. We should add that to the list of stuff to pick up."

I pulled out my phone and typed it into my notes.

"Let's check the banister," she said. "I want to make sure all the lights are working."

As I followed her up the staircase, I inspected each white bulb embedded in the garland. Red bows had been placed at every measured foot all the way up to the top. "Looks good to me."

"Now the tree." Ruby pointed back downstairs.

"It's easier to look at it from up here," I replied.

The fifteen-foot fake fir tree stood in the corner also covered in white lights, a few bows, and many ornaments, some of which I had made as a child. Others had been given to me by special people in my life. All had deep meaning for me. I'd also found some lemon-scented car fresheners to hang on the bottom branches. My hope had been they would repel my cranky tabby, Elvira, and to my utter shock, it seemed to be working. She'd approached the tree a couple of times but turned the other way once she got close. Not a very holiday-like scent, but it was better than her climbing the tree and taking it down.

As I looked over my living room, a sense of peace blanketed me and I smiled. I loved Christmas.

"You need to invite more people to the party," Ruby said. "We want to have the biggest rager in town!"

"I'm fine with our small guest list," I said. Ragers were *not* my thing. "Besides, I don't know that many people."

I tended to be an introverted homebody, but while alive, Ruby had been the life of every party and had known everyone in town.

"Just get out more!" she urged. "Go to the bar! Join a club!"

"I like my life just the way it is," I replied as I hurried down the staircase. "I'm not arguing with you."

"You better not leave me here!" Ruby yelled from right behind me. "Don't even try!"

"Have I ever left you behind?" I asked, grabbing my purse. "Besides, we agreed we'd go together today."

"That's a dumb question. Of course you've left me. Or at least, you tried."

I stared at my ghost for a long moment and recalled she was right. When we were inside our home, Ruby roamed freely. Once we left the four walls, she couldn't go more than fifteen feet away from me. Somehow, we were tethered together by an unseen "leash," as she liked to call it.

Sometimes I raced out of the house in order get a little time to myself. Guilty as charged.

"Let's go!" Ruby yelled as we made our way to the back door where I stopped to don my coat.

We headed to the SUV and I slid in. The drive to town remained uneventful, except for Ruby's singing. Once we arrived, finding a parking spot became a nightmare.

"Everyone's doing their shopping!" Ruby squealed. "I love this time of year!"

I finally discovered an empty space behind Joyous Jewels, the local jewelry store featuring a lot of turquoise, silver and Native American pieces.

As Ruby and I walked over to the main drag, she hummed and spun around in circles. "We need to find some good gag gifts for the white elephant exchange," she said. "That's always a hoot when someone ends up with something ridiculous."

I stopped at the Joyous Jewels window which had a painting of a Christmas tree and twinkling lights around the frame. The glimmering pieces of jewelry caught my eye even though I never wore any. I glanced down at my mood ring—

the only piece I did wear besides my earrings—and noted the color as dark blue. Happiness. Yes, things were going well for me. I waved at the owner, Merry, and continued on my way.

All the stores had participated in the decoration festivities and some even had Christmas music piped out onto the walkways in front of their stores. Ruby gave a running commentary of her opinion on the decorations, what people were wearing, and anything she found interesting.

"Oh! Look! A Santa figurine! It's perfect, Bernie!" Ruby exclaimed as she pointed at a store window. "But that man's sweater... ugh. I bet his grandma knitted that thinking she was doing him a favor. He's probably wearing it to be nice to her. I bet that ends up in a donation bin."

Yes, the jolly Santa figurine would fit in with the village perfectly. And frankly, there were a lot of men around with awful sweaters, so I wasn't sure which one she meant. "Let's go in," I murmured.

We went inside to purchase the figurine and I picked up a few decoration replacement bulbs just in case one did go out. My motto: better to be prepared than sorry.

After waiting in line for a bit, we exited the store. A man I'd seen earlier at Joyous Jewels stood outside and we exchanged smiles as I passed. Tall with dirty, dark hair, his overly large coat hung on his thin frame.

Ruby and I walked by a few other stores and she continued her running commentary. This store did a beautiful job of decorating. That store should have tried harder. Why was that woman wearing flipflops in winter? The man over there was going to have back problems from carrying all his wife's packages. I half-listened as I took in the window displays.

As we strolled by Fiona's Flowers, I caught a glimpse in the window. The tall guy I'd noticed earlier was following me. "Let's go in here," I whispered as I opened the door.

"Why? No one wants flowers for a white elephant gift exchange! Where's the fun in that?"

As I pretended to study the different bouquets, I glanced up at the window. Sure enough, he stood just outside as if he waited for me.

"You're right," I whispered. "No one wants flowers. Let's leave."

"That was fast," Ruby said. "Glad you listened to reasoning. Where should we head to next?"

"Let's keep looking," I whispered, checking over my shoulder every few minutes. The man was still present, although he didn't seem to be paying me much attention. Was he following me or not? After being mixed up in several murders, I'd learned to always be aware of the happenings around me.

"Pizza socks, Bernie!" Ruby exclaimed, pointing at a window display. "We need pizza socks!"

I couldn't agree more.

We found a plethora of quirky gifts in the store, aptly named Perfect Presents and Parties . A Public Toilet Survival Kit that included wipes, latex gloves, and a toilet seat cover. Elephant Salt and Pepper shakers. A Dinosaur Kale Growing Kit.

"Can you imagine Gunner wearing the pizza socks?" Ruby asked. Despite being surrounded by people who couldn't see or hear my ghost speaking to me, I laughed and received a few odd glares. Gunner, a cop who'd been under-cover for five years with a biker gang, stood over six feet tall and had the build of a military tank. Pizza socks on him would be hysterical.

After grabbing all my finds, I walked over to the checkout and stood in line, Ruby right next to me.

"Do we have everything?" she asked. "I think we do."

I checked my list, mentally counted my gifts and nodded,

but didn't answer. It would appear I was having a full conversation with myself to everyone else in the store.

After paying cash, we headed back to the car. I glanced over my shoulder a couple of times and didn't see my stalker. Right before we reached Joyous Jewels again, I found myself face-to-face with him.

"Excuse me," he grumbled as he tried to side-step me while looking over my head at the crowd behind me.

I attempted to move out of his way, but we ended up stepping the same direction, then engaging in the awkward dance of two people trying to avoid each other, but only succeeding in remaining in each other's path.

His focus remained beyond me and I finally stood in place. Our shoulders bumped as he hurried by, not bothering to apologize.

"Rude," I muttered, determined not to let him ruin my perfect day. When we arrived at the car, I slid in, glad to be free of the throngs of people.

"That was so much fun!" Ruby squealed. "I adore Christmas shopping!"

Usually I did as well, but despite my attempts to forget the man and enjoy the day, I couldn't stop thinking about him. Had he been following me? It certainly seemed that way. The fact I'd spotted him outside almost every store we visited caused me worry.

And my worry turned to panic when I arrived home to find my wallet missing.

CHAPTER 2

"THAT GUY I thought was following me must have taken it!" I yelled as I glanced at the contents of my purse scattered across the kitchen island. "When he bumped me! He must have somehow grabbed my wallet!"

"It's okay, honey," Ruby said, running her hand over my arm. Goosebumps appeared as she did so and a shiver ran down my spine. Her touch always felt like ice had been laid on my skin. "It's just a few calls to the bank and a trip to the Department of Motor Vehicles to get a new license."

"I should've known he'd pull something like that," I said, groaning. "The DMV is the worst."

Ruby smiled and blew me a kiss. "Maybe with the holidays getting a new license won't be such a long wait. People are concentrating on other things."

As the scent of lavender and marijuana—what Ruby had smelled like while alive—engulfed me, I sighed. The trip to the DMV would have to wait until after the party. Until then, I'd have to be extra careful while driving so I didn't get pulled over or end up in an accident.

"Besides, I went seven years with an invalid license

without a problem," Ruby said. "No one checks the date on those things anymore. It's not like you have to do it right away."

Of course, this bit of advice came from the woman who was arrested for streaking down a golf course. And drinking tequila naked at the Bell Rock Vortex. All while in her seventies. The list of laws she broke while younger stretched extensively.

A knock sounded on the front door, thankfully bringing the conversation to an end. I hurried over and opened it to find Henry, my handyman.

"Hi, Henry," I said. "Come on in."

"You should consider dating him," Ruby said. "Handymen are very good with their hands, if you know what I mean."

Pursing my lips, I did my best to ignore her and the blush crawling up my cheeks. She'd died of a heart attack while in bed with her handyman. Relief swept through me when she disappeared, laughing hysterically at my embarrassment.

In his thirties and very married, Henry's black hair sprouted from his red baseball cap bearing his company name, Handyman Henry. Not very creative, but there was no doubt about his profession. A thick black beard covered his jaw. His weathered, calloused hand gripped mine as he smiled. "Nice to see you again, Bernie."

"You too. Thanks for coming on short notice. How're the kids? And Judy?"

"As good as four kids under the age of eight can be," he replied, glancing around the living room. "And Judy's fine, thanks for asking. Looks like you're in the Christmas spirit."

"Oh, yes," I said. "My favorite time of the year. I tend to go overboard with the decorations."

"It appears Santa came early, too," he said, pointing at the couch where I'd dumped all my presents.

"Yes. I'm having a party and a white elephant gift exchange."

"Sounds nice," he murmured, then turned to me. "Do you need anything done in here?"

I shook my head. "Only outside."

"Why don't you show me and I'll get started?"

After stepping out and explaining where I wanted the lights to go, I hurried back to the kitchen and phoned the bank to cancel my credit card. During that time, my friend Darla had called.

"Hi!" I said when she answered, putting her on speakerphone.

"Hey, Bernie. I was wondering if you could come by the diner for a bit. I'm working on new recipes for the party and I wanted you to do a taste test."

I glanced at my packages that needed wrapping. They could wait until I got home. Henry would leave an invoice for me, so there was no reason for me to hang around. "Sure. I can be there in about twenty minutes?"

"Perfect. Oh, and can you bring Ruby?"

Darla was one of the few people I had told about my ghost. Bonus points to her for not thinking I was out of my mind. "Of course."

"I understand I'm in high demand," Ruby said, appearing next to me. "It's exhausting being so dang popular." She raised her hand to her forehead and sighed dramatically.

"See you in a bit, Darla," I said. After hanging up, I turned to my grandmother. "Come on, drama llama, let's go."

I admired the red rocks of Sedona as we drove to Darling's Diner. Tall, rugged and the color of rust, they provided a beautiful landscape to our town and I couldn't imagine going a day without appreciating their magical splendor.

After parking in the lot between Darling's Diner and

11

Jumping Jack Jeep Tours, I exited the vehicle and headed into the restaurant. The hostess waved and motioned for me to head to the kitchen where I found Darla among the stainless-steel tables, gas stoves, and fryers.

"Hey, Bernie!" my friend greeted me as we embraced. In her thirties—the same age as me—we'd been friends since I moved to town. "How are things going?"

"Good. Everything's coming together nicely." Despite the party being my idea, the butterflies of anxiety still tickled my belly. I wanted everything to be perfect.

"And now we need to go over the party menu," Darla said, tucking a blonde lock of hair behind her ear as she looked to my right, then my left. "Hi Ruby! I keep hoping that one day I'll be able to see her."

"Hey, Darla!" Ruby replied, smiling, then she turned to me. "I just love it when your friends speak to me."

Darla suffered from schizophrenia but seemed to be doing well. In all my time knowing her, I'd never seen her so happy and peaceful. Besides her medication, Jack, who owned Jumping Jack Jeep Tours next door, most likely had a lot to do with her calm disposition. They'd been dating a few months and both were very happy.

"I know you wanted to keep things simple, but I was hoping you'd say yes after tasting the Beef Wellington with grilled asparagus," Darla said shyly.

"Beef Wellington!" I exclaimed. "Seriously?"

"Yes! I want to do a big sit-down dinner, Bernie! The planning and cooking... it's been so much fun. I know it's your party and we agreed on a simple meal, but I wanted to try something different. Something a little fancier."

I had imagined appetizers and finger sandwiches. After mentally tabulating the chairs at my dining room table, I didn't find a problem. Everyone would fit and I'd never eaten

Beef Wellington before. "If you're up for it, Darla, then you can serve whatever you'd like."

"What about our dance party?" Ruby asked. "Is this going to turn into some hoity-toity thing where everyone sits around sipping after-dinner tea?"

"No, we'll still have our dance party," I said.

When I visited Ruby in my younger years, she'd pull out a chest of clothes and we'd dress up for a specific time-period, move the furniture in the living room, and blast music until late at night. We had more disco parties than I could count.

"Oh, good." Ruby sniffed. "Since I can't eat, I find all this talk of food particularly cruel."

"Then just ignore us," I said. "You wanted to come and you knew we would be discussing the food."

"I know, but I can still feel sorry for myself."

Turning back to Darla, I smiled. "Let's see what you've got."

She reached into the oven and pulled out a prepared plate of Beef Wellington, grilled asparagus, and mashed potatoes. My mouth watered as I inhaled the delicious scents.

"That looks amazing," I murmured, wiping the corner of my mouth, afraid I'd drool.

"Take a seat," she said, pointing to the small table in the corner.

I sat down and she placed the plate in front of me, then took the chair across from me. As I cut into the Beef Wellington, she studied my every move. I suddenly feared it would be awful and I wouldn't be able to hide my disdain.

Thankfully, the food almost melted in my mouth and before I knew it, I'd cleared my plate.

"I'm going to take your silence and the fact you practically inhaled everything as a good sign," Darla said, chuckling.

"Yeah, she reminded me of my Hoover vacuum I used to

use," Ruby said. "That thing would suck up a small child if needed."

"That was delicious," I said, slightly embarrassed at my lack of etiquette. "Amazing."

"So I can serve it at your party?" Darla asked, her eyes dancing with excitement.

"Of course you can!" I replied. "Now that I've tasted it, I'd be upset if you didn't!"

"I can't wait for this shindig," Darla said. She took my plate and walked it over to the sink, then poured two cups of coffee and set them on a tray with cream and sugar. "It's going to be so much fun."

"Yes. It's going to be small, but I think it will be great." In total, I had six guests including myself. If you counted the ghosts that would be present, there'd be eight. My boyfriend, Deputy Adam Gallagher, had a ghost living with him as well. Fortunately for him, his spirit, Ned, was nothing like Ruby. Instead, he liked to keep to himself and Adam couldn't see or hear him—but I could. Ever since I was hit by lightning, I'd become some sort of ghost whisperer and I'd yet to decide if it was a good or bad thing. On one hand, I could see ghosts! On the other hand, could I really? Or had the lightning strike scrambled my brains and I was imagining all these spirits? This was a question I pondered often.

Darla took a sip of her coffee. "What have you been up to today?"

"We went shopping for the white elephant gift exchange," I said as I poured cream into my coffee. "And, I had my wallet stolen."

"Oh, no! How did that happen?"

"I swear this guy was following me," I replied. I gave her a blow-by-blow of where I'd seen him and how he hung outside the flower shop as if he waited for me. "Then he disappeared. A little later, Ruby and I were walking back to the car and he bumped into me. When we got home, I realized my wallet was gone."

"So you think he took it when he knocked into you?"

I nodded. "It's the only time I could've lost it."

"That's too bad. Did you call your credit card company?"

"Yes. Now I need to get a new license and I hate the DMV."

Darla laughed and shook her head. "I've never heard anyone say they enjoyed going, Bernie. It's one of the ugly things in life one must do."

As we chatted, Ruby remained so quiet, I almost forgot she had come with me. However, when Darla's boyfriend, Jack, walked in, Ruby came alive. Well, as alive as she could, considering she was dead.

"Hello, there, Mr. Dimples," she purred. "Aren't you looking sexy today in those greasy jeans?"

Jack owned Jumping Jack Jeep Tours next door, which, aptly named, offered Jeep tours of the Sedona area. He did most of his own repairs and could be found covered in grease or dirt at any given time. Ruby also considered him the best-looking man in Arizona, and she might be correct. With his wavy brown hair and deep green eyes, he was handsome. Combined with his bright smile where his dimples became more pronounced—hence her nickname for him—he became magazine-worthy material.

Darla stood and kissed him. "I should've realized you'd show up in time for dessert."

"Oh, she's so lucky," Ruby said, sighing. "If I were alive, I'd give him a kiss he'd never forget."

"I've never missed dessert, Darla," he replied, his eyes twinkling. "How are you doing, Bernie?"

"Good," I said, so thankful he couldn't hear my ghost. "Your girlfriend is going to make me put on weight."

He grabbed his taut stomach with each hand. "You and me both."

I rolled my eyes as Darla opened the fridge and pulled out three plates. "We've got a chocolate tart, a cinnamon apple pie, or a creme brûlée."

"Can't we have all three at the dinner?" Jack asked, sitting down at the table. "After all, it is a Christmas celebration."

Darla handed us each a fork and the three of us tasted each treat.

"They're all delicious, Darla," I said, groaning. "I can't choose."

"You have to vote for one," Darla chided. "Which one was your favorite?"

I really couldn't answer. "I'll let Jack decide." As I stood, I stretched my arms over my head, suddenly exhausted. Must have been all the calories I'd consumed. "So, I'll see you two tomorrow night?"

"I'll be there around four, if that's okay," Darla said.

"Of course. Are you still planning dinner at six?"

"Yes."

"We'll see you then!" Jack said. "Oh, wait! Is Ruby with you?"

I nodded and grabbed my purse off the back of the chair.

"Tell her I say hello."

"And tell him those jeans hug his tush nicely," Ruby said.

"I will, Jack," I said before hurrying out of the diner with my ghost in tow. Would there ever be a time when she didn't embarrass me? And why did I allow it? Only I could hear her. Perhaps I feared that one day, they would.

Adam, my boyfriend, called as I drove through town.

"You shouldn't be on the phone while driving, Bernie," he said after we exchanged greetings.

"I'm on Bluetooth. Totally hands-free."

"You should still be concentrating on the road. I've seen a lot of accidents with Bluetooth in use."

"I wanted to talk to you," I countered. "Besides, I'm almost home. I could drive this road with my eyes closed. Are you coming over?"

"Yes. I was calling to let you know I'll be there in about half an hour."

I pulled into the lot behind my house and turned off the car. "I'll see you then!"

"Let's go around front and see what Henry did!" Ruby exclaimed as I ended the call.

When we reached the front of the house, I examined the area where I'd asked him to string the lights. They hung evenly and would be pretty once lit. Everything was on a timer and previously when I'd messed with the settings, I'd accidently programmed the device to go off at four in the morning. I'd leave it alone for now. I went inside and made a mental note to check the display after dark.

After grabbing my wrapping paper and locating my scissors and tape, I went into the living room, turned on some Christmas music, and sat down to wrap my presents.

I gasped as I sank into the cushions, panic constricting my chest while my stomach curled with disgust.

They were gone.

CHAPTER 3

THE GOOD THING about dating a cop was that he arrived right away. The bad thing was that he went directly into what I called "cop mode" and started interrogating me as if I wasn't his girlfriend but some criminal he'd arrested.

"Have you checked out the rest of the house?" he asked, his voice brisk and all business. "To make sure no one's hiding?"

"Ruby made me sit down here and she went through all the rooms upstairs," I mumbled. "She couldn't find anyone."

"I'm going to do a quick sweep for myself," he replied. "No offense, Ruby. I believe you looked, but I'll feel better if I do as well."

"None taken, copper," Ruby said when Adam ran upstairs. "Do what you need to do to unknot your boxers."

A few moments later, Adam returned. "Do you know where they entered from?" he asked, examining the front door. "Did you lock up before you left?"

"I think so," I grumbled as I took a seat on my couch and stared at the Christmas tree. "I don't know how they got in, but I know who did it."

"Who?"

"The guy who stole my wallet downtown," I said. "He had my license, so he knew my address. He's probably been watching the house and waiting for me to leave so he could break in uninterrupted. He saw I had a bunch of packages."

Adam hurried over and kneeled in front of me. "Your wallet was stolen?"

Angry tears welled in my eyes as I told him the story. "He was following me and probably saw a lone woman out loaded down with shopping bags as an easy target."

He sat down next to me and pulled out a notebook. "Can you describe this guy?"

"Tall, thin, greasy dark hair," I said. "He resembles the grinch. Except he was white, not green."

Adam sighed and jotted down my description. "I'm going to check the back door and downstairs windows."

"There weren't any broken windows when I looked," Ruby said, sitting on the couch across from me. "I think if that jerk had gotten in that way, you'd feel a breeze. Do you?"

I shook my head. "Nothing."

"He must've gotten in through the back door, then."

My tabby cat, Elvira, stalked into the room from the kitchen and meowed to announce her presence.

"Come here," I said, patting the cushion next to me. "Come give me some love. I need it."

Instead, she narrowed her gaze, lifted her nose in the air, and walked up the stairs. I swear the only reason the cat stuck around was because of Ruby, whom she loved. On the other hand, I—the one who fed her, cleaned her litterbox and desperately wanted to snuggle her—was someone she barely tolerated.

"The party will be fine without the gifts," Ruby said. "Tell everyone what happened. No one will care."

"I know," I muttered. "But *I* care. I wanted the party to be perfect."

"There's no such thing, Bernie." Ruby sighed. "I don't know how many times I need to tell you to stop aiming for perfection because it's never going to happen. Just accept things as they are, throw your shoulders back, smile, and take it all in stride."

Easy for her to say. She hadn't been planning the party for a month.

Adam strode back into the room. "They came in through the door in the kitchen," he said, jotting down something in his notebook. "There're scratches on the lock and the door-frame I don't recall seeing before."

"Did they pick it, or just bust it?" I asked. Did I need to call Henry back to fix the lock?

"It'll hold, but definitely replace it." He sat down next to me and took my hand in his. "In fact, I'd like for you to swap out all the locks for something with a deadbolt. They all look pretty old. I can do it for you, if you'd like my help."

Laying my head on his shoulder, I took a ragged breath. Another thing to add to my to-do list.

"I'm going to have to grab my laptop and make a report," Adam continued. "I'll also check if there are any other similar incidents. Maybe he's got other houses he's hit. It's probably a good idea to send someone to patrol downtown and see if they can spot this grinch guy."

Elvira stood at the top of the stairs watching us through a narrowed gaze, her tail swishing back and forth.

"I'll be right back," Adam said. He stood and kissed my forehead, then strode out the front door to his car to retrieve his laptop.

When he returned, he sat down next to me again and typed up the report. "I don't see anything in here resembling your experience," he murmured. "A couple of drunk drivers, a small fire from a candle, and a couple of cars broken into. Nothing about a woman being followed and her wallet being stolen."

"He'll do it again," I said. "He was a pro. Otherwise he wouldn't have been able to lift my wallet from my purse without me knowing it."

"It was unzipped?"

I nodded.

"You should always keep your purse zipped when in a crowded area," Adam lectured. "In fact, just keep it zipped at all times so it becomes a habit."

"A little late for that advice, copper," Ruby muttered. "And just a bit patronizing if you ask me."

Biting my tongue, I stood and hurried into the kitchen to fetch a glass of water. I agreed with Ruby. If I didn't put some space between the two of us, I'd most likely say something I'd regret. Adam and I had dated for months, then broken up because of my own dumb actions. I didn't want to rock the boat anymore now that we were back together, especially over something so stupid.

Of course, I knew my purse should've been zipped. It was like telling someone who had tripped to watch their step. Irritating and unnecessary.

When I finished my water, I returned to the living room and smiled. I'd bring the conversation up another time.

"So everything else is ready for the party?" he asked, closing his laptop.

"Yes. Darla's making an amazing meal and all the lights are finally hung outside."

"We're all looking forward to it, Bernie," he said, wrapping his arm around my shoulder. "The house looks great, by the way."

Elvira meowed and I glanced up at her again. She stalked over to the banister, keeping her gaze firmly on me.

When she jumped onto the railing, I shot to my feet and yelled, "Don't even think about it!"

"Uh oh," Ruby said. "It's a test of wills and I know who's going to win. And it's not the lemon-scented air fresheners."

"Elvira!" I screamed as she readied herself, her tail swishing again as all the muscles in her hindlegs twitched. "Don't! Please... don't do it!"

Time seemed to stop as my cat lunged through the air Superman-style and hit her mark—my Christmas tree—with incredible precision. The ornaments rattled, some crashing to the floor and breaking into pieces. The tree swayed as Elvira batted at the lights and other decorations.

"Dang it! You stupid cat! Get down from there!" I yelled.

Adam raced over and reached to steady the tree, but it was too late. It came crashing down on top of him, taking him to the floor. Elvira leaped again and cleared the disaster, then sat down to admire her handiwork.

"Copper down! Copper down! Mayday! Mayday!" Ruby yelled waving her hands in the air while I pulled the tree off Adam.

"Are you okay?" I said, dropping to my knees beside him. Spatters of blood surrounded his head, seeping into my rug.

"I think so," he muttered, closing his eyes. As he reached for the back of his head, I noted blood on his knuckles.

"Run, cat, run!" Ruby yelled. "She'll make you into a pair of gloves for this debacle!"

"You're bleeding," I said. "Let me get a cloth."

I strode into the kitchen and noted Elvira had taken Ruby's advice and gone to hide. A good thing, because I was so angry, I debated taking her to the shelter.

With a slew of curses, I wetted a towel and hurried back into the living room. Adam had stood but I noted blood pooling at his neck.

"I think you need to head to the emergency room," I said,

placing the cloth on the back of his head. "You may need stitches. You're bleeding pretty bad."

Glancing around the floor, I found so much glass and broken ornaments, I was surprised more damage hadn't been done to him.

"I'll be fine," he muttered, bending over to grab the tree. As he tried to set it upright, the plastic core snapped in half.

"Uh oh," Ruby said. "Between the broken tree and the stolen gifts, I have a feeling Christmas is canceled."

"You need to go get that cut checked out," I said as tears welled in my eyes and I ignored my ghost. "Let me drive you."

"Really, it's—"

Tired of my day and everything that had happened, I snapped. "Quit being such a man!" I yelled, my hands clenched at my sides. "I can practically see your brains that cut's so deep! You need stitches!"

"Well, someone's not happy," Ruby scoffed. "You need to calm down."

"Don't tell me to calm down!" I screamed.

"I didn't," Adam said, his eyes wide. "You're scaring me, Bernie."

"I wasn't talking to you!" I marched into the kitchen to retrieve my purse and coat, then I returned to the living room and pointed toward the back door. "Now get in my car!"

"I'll stay home," Ruby called as I followed Adam. "This doesn't seem like a fun trip, and I hate hospitals."

My hands shook as I jammed the key into the ignition. Thankfully, Adam remained silent as I drove. I took some deep breaths and tried to calm myself. Of course, I worried about him. Glancing over, I could see the soaked cloth was leaking all over my car seat. Just another thing to deal with.

I pulled up in front of the emergency room and walked him in even though he insisted he didn't need any help. The on-duty guard told me to move my car but I just glared at him and muttered for him to mind his own business. Hopefully he wouldn't ask for the ID I no longer possessed.

"We'll get you in quick," the nurse said, eyeing the bloody rag with distaste. "Just take a seat for a minute or two."

"You'll need to go park your car now," the guard said, his voice gentle and quiet as if trying to talk a toddler out of a tantrum. "Or I'll have to have it towed."

I strode out of the building feeling like a child about ready to throw myself down on the ground and scream and cry. First the gifts had been stolen. Then my cat had destroyed my living room. A trip to the emergency department. Not to mention the blood I needed to clean up in my house and car.

Laying my forehead against the steering wheel, I allowed the tears to flow freely. My Christmas spirit seeped away like water through a crack in the pavement. Anger at my unknown burglar and my cat replaced it and consumed me, along with utter exhaustion. I didn't have the fortitude to put any more energy into the holiday.

Ruby was right: Christmas was canceled.

CHAPTER 4

LATE THAT NIGHT, I drove Adam back to my house. I'd been right: he'd required stitches and the doctor also wanted me to watch him for a concussion.

I had set my phone alarm to repeat every two hours, but despite my exhaustion, I didn't need it. I barely slept as I worried for Adam. From the white rocking chair in my bedroom, I wrapped myself in a blanket and monitored him closely as he lay under the yellow comforter, his soft snores filling the room. As the morning sun rays peeked through the window, he woke with a light headache and soreness around the stitches but seemed happy once he was up and settled in the kitchen while I made coffee and toast.

Since arriving home the previous evening, I'd avoided the living room and hadn't seen my horrible cat. Even though I wanted to strangle her, I set out her food. Ruby had also disappeared. Most likely she'd gone to her tunnel, a place she said led to Heaven. It was dark except for the illumination at the end of it. According to her, she'd tried numerous times to get to the light, but she never could. It remained out of her grasp and both of us figured Heaven wasn't quite ready for Ruby, leaving her trapped on this plane.

As Adam and I sat quietly in the kitchen sipping our coffee, I tried to pretend yesterday never happened, although I'd have to face the mess in my living room at some point.

"How are you feeling today?" Adam asked.

"Tired. I barely slept."

"Thanks for watching out for me. I think I'm fine, though."

"I'm glad," I said, grabbing his hand. "I was worried."

A knock sounded at the front door. With a groan, I hauled myself up from the barstool and shuffled over to answer it. I'd closed my reservation app and hung out my No Vacancy sign, both virtually and physically, until after Christmas. Some people obviously didn't pay attention to such things. Or perhaps my ugly Christmas sweater had arrived just in time for the party I was about to cancel.

I kept my gaze firmly on the floor as I walked through the living room, not quite ready to face the disaster. More coffee and a hardening of my heart would be needed before I could take a broom to the mess and scrub the blood out of my carpet and hardwood floors.

To my utter shock, my friends Jezebel and Gunner graced my doorway.

"What are you guys doing here?" I asked, stepping aside to let them in.

"Adam texted us," Jezebel replied as she took me into a firm embrace. "Said you had a bit of an accident here and needed some help cleaning up."

I finally turned around and studied the scene of the cat-crime.

The tree lay in the middle of the living room, the top half crooked at an odd angle while the bottom half still had a few lights blinking. Broken ornaments and glass surrounded it.

Some decorations remained intact on the upward facing side of the tree and scattered around the living room, but not many. I hadn't noticed it the previous night, but some picture frames from the fireplace mantel had also gotten caught up in the melee. Adam's blood dotted the crime scene. My stomach turned as I took it all in. My Christmas tree and its ornaments had been precious to me because of the memories they held. As I studied the mess, I had the urge to vomit and cry all at once.

"Wow. Elvira did that?" Gunner asked as he crossed his thick arms over his chest. "I'm a bit impressed."

"Yeah, it kind of looks like a tornado came through here," Jezebel agreed. "Maybe some hurricane force winds. At least she left the Christmas village alone."

But she hadn't. At some point, she'd gotten into the Christmas village and knocked over my new Santa figurine, which lay shattered on the floor.

I realized that Elvira had been angry at my attempts to keep her away from the tree by hanging lemon car fresheners around the bottom branches. And it had worked. She hated the lemon scent. However, I never imagined she'd go to such lengths for revenge and I didn't know if I could ever forgive her.

"She was definitely going after the tree," Adam said as he strolled in. "Dang cat jumped from the upstairs railing to the tree and everything came down."

"Let's see *your* damage," Gunner said. Adam turned around to reveal a bald spot where the doctor had shaved him and a nice line of stitches. Gunner studied them a moment then shook his head. "All from a cat. Who knew they could cause so much destruction? What did you hit?"

He'd obviously never owned a cat if he didn't know the level of damage they were capable of.

"I'm not sure," Adam said. "Maybe the table on the way

down? Or it could've been any of the broken ornaments. They did find glass in the cut. I didn't feel anything until Bernie noticed I was bleeding."

"And now?" Gunner asked.

"Slight headache," Adam said with a sigh. "And my pride's hurt for being bested by a cat. I should've been able to save the tree."

Jezebel turned to me. "How are *you* holding up?" Her brow creased with concern as she tucked a blonde lock behind her ear.

"I'm tired. I was really worried about Adam last night. I had to watch him for signs of concussion."

"From the looks of it, he's going to be fine," she said, patting my shoulder. "Trust me. I've had worse injuries."

Jezebel had once wanted to become a professional MMA fighter, but she was never quite good enough. As she strode into the kitchen, her jeans hugged her thick, muscular legs. She'd kept up her physique even though she'd quit fighting. Instead, she ran Tip 'Em Back, a dive bar on the edge of town, and taught self-defense. With my yoga-loving peaceful ways, I found it strange to have a friend who embraced violence so easily, but I'd learned that sometimes, violence needed to be met with violence... or at least the ability to defend myself. After almost being tossed down a stairwell headfirst, I'd signed up for her class and we'd quickly become friends.

Ruby appeared next to me and grinned when Jezebel returned with a glass of water. "Hey, Jezzy! In spite of what it did to you, don't you love nature?"

"That's mean!" I scolded. "Be nice, Ruby!"

While alive, Ruby had been friends with Jezebel's grand-mother. The two spent a lot of time together and had a tradition of greeting each other with insults.

"Tell her what I said!" Ruby yelled, jumping up and down, clapping her hands. "She'll love it!"

I repeated the offense and Jezebel burst out laughing. "Ruby, I refuse to have a battle of wits with someone who's unarmed."

"Oh! Good one," Gunner called. "She got you there, Ruby!"

Despite the mess and my profound sadness, I found myself chuckling along with everyone else. Having been under a cloud of despair since yesterday, the levity of the moment was a much-needed reprieve.

"Can you grab us a few brooms, a vacuum, and some garbage bags?" Gunner asked. "We'll have this cleaned up in no time."

As I hurried into the hallway to fetch everything from the closet, tears sprang into my eyes. I was so grateful for my friends. The mess wouldn't have taken me long to clean up, but emotionally, it would have been difficult at best. Many of the ornaments carried great memories for me. My heart ached at the thought of trashing them.

"Go sit down in the kitchen," Jezebel instructed when I returned with the supplies. "Take a load off and try to relax."

Gunner winked at me as he took the vacuum. With his thick black beard, bald head, and sheer size, he'd frightened me the first time I'd met him. As a cop, he'd been undercover in a motorcycle club, but I hadn't been aware of that little detail. I'd accused the gang of being involved in a murder and Gunner had threatened me in hopes of protecting me by making me stay away from the club. When I hadn't, Adam and Jezebel had to tell me his secret. Even though I'd almost blown his cover, we'd become fast friends once the murder was solved.

As my friends and Adam cleaned up my memories, I checked my email in the kitchen and had another cup of coffee.

My insurance was due. Did I want to renew my home warranty? Then a customer begging me to open for Christmas so she didn't have to have her in-laws stay at her house over the holiday. I typed back a nice, but firm, note. My bed and breakfast would be closed until the twenty-eighth.

Jezebel walked in moments later with a large garbage bag and headed out the back door to dump it in the bin. When she returned, she sat down. "It looks like someone tried to break into your house. The back door's all scratched up."

"They tried and succeeded," I said. "And stole all the gifts for the white elephant exchange."

"Oh, no! Were you home?"

"They waited until I was gone. I know who did it. Some guy was following me while I was shopping, and then he took my wallet."

"You really did have one heck of a bad day yesterday," Jezebel said, shaking her head.

Gunner entered carrying half the tree. "We couldn't resuscitate it," he said. "The middle is snapped in half. You'll have to get another one."

"I set all the ornaments that survived on the couch, Bernie," Adam said, hauling the other half. "We'll get you a new tree today."

No, we wouldn't.

"Should you be doing that?' I asked. "The doctor told you to take it easy for a few days."

Adam smiled and rolled his eyes. "Honey, I'm fine. Really."

Not listening to doctor's orders... Typical man.

As the two men made their way out the back door, I said, "I just want to cancel the party, Jezebel. I don't have a tree. I don't have any gifts. My Christmas spirit has fled the building."

"We don't need all that stuff," she countered. "Christmas is about spending time with friends and family, not about the decorations and the gifts. Besides, what's Darla going to do with all the food if we don't eat it?"

"Donate to a shelter," I grumbled. "I'm not in the mood for a party."

"That's because you're tired and you had one awful day yesterday," Jezebel replied. "You'll feel differently after you get some sleep."

Ruby appeared directly behind the woman, her hands on her hips. "And now I'm the Ghost of Christmas Present. Quit with the pity party. So some stuff went wrong. That doesn't mean Christmas should be canceled."

I didn't have the energy to argue with either of them.

When my phone shrilled, I almost dropped it on the floor it scared me so badly.

"It's Darla," I said when her name popped up on the screen. I answered quickly. "Hello?"

"Hey! It's me!"

Although she sounded chipper, I knew something was wrong. I could hear her trying to disguise it in her voice. I placed my elbow on the table and my forehead in my hand. Another wave of exhaustion rolled through me and I sighed while closing my eyes. "What's wrong, Darla?"

"Why do you think something's wrong?" she asked, her voice high and tight.

"Just tell me," I said. "What happened?"

CHAPTER 5

"You're never going to believe me, but one of my refrigerators went down last night," Darla said. "It was the one that held tonight's meal."

Pursing my lips, I stared at the floor, believing every word. Obviously, the universe did not want me to have my Christmas party. It wanted me miserable during my favorite time of the year.

"No problem, Darla," I said. "I'm going to cancel the party anyway."

"No! Don't because of this! I can put together the original menu—some finger sandwiches, chips, dip... I'll have everything whipped up in no time."

"It's not just the food," I said, sitting back and meeting Jezebel's gaze. "After I got back from your place yesterday, I discovered my house had been broken into and they took all my white elephant gifts."

"Oh, my word!" Darla exclaimed. "Do they know who did it?"

"I think it was that guy I told you about who followed me and stole my wallet. He had my address and probably waited until I left before breaking in. He saw me carrying all my gifts and knew I had a big haul."

"That's terrible," Darla replied. "What's happening to people's Christmas spirit?"

Really good question. "Then last night, Elvira took down the tree." Despite my efforts, I couldn't hold back the tears. "She jumped from the banister onto the tree and it toppled over. Adam tried to rescue it, but he fell and I had to take him to the hospital to get stiches in his head."

Darla remained quiet for a long moment. "I'm so sorry, Bernie. I know how much those ornaments meant to you."

"Yes." I wiped my cheeks as Jezebel fetched a box of tissue. "Jezebel and Gunner are here cleaning up for me."

"Is Adam going to be okay?"

When he and Gunner strolled in from outside, they spoke in low tones, then returned to the living room. "He seems fine. They had to shave a strip of his hair to clean the wound. It looks pretty silly."

"I'm glad he wasn't hurt worse. What a relief."

"So, as you can imagine, I'm not in any mood to celebrate Christmas," I said. "In fact, I'd like to go to bed and wake up after New Year's."

"I'm working on changing her attitude," Jezebel said loudly so Darla could hear her. "We're *all* going to celebrate Christmas."

"No, I'm not," I said. "If you guys want to get together, fine. I'm staying home. Christmas is canceled."

"Put Jezebel on the phone," Darla said. "I need to plan with her. I know you've had a rough couple of days, but you're acting like the Grinch. You planned your little heart out and now Jezebel and I will take it from here. "

I handed the phone to my friend and announced I would take a shower. They didn't seem to understand that I had absolutely no intention of participating in any type of celebration. Forgetting tomorrow was Christmas Eve sounded like the best course of action for me. Perhaps Darla was right. *I* was the Grinch, but I couldn't seem to get past my string of bad Christmas luck.

After my shower, I slipped on my sweats and sweatshirt. Staring at my bed, I suddenly became so tired, I didn't think I could take another step. I slipped under the comforter and closed my eyes, inhaling Adam's scent on the pillow which consisted of his shampoo and disinfectant. Just before sleep overtook me, Elvira snuggled into my neck and purred loudly.

"I hate you," I whispered, yet I reached up and stroked her back.

She meowed and darkness engulfed me.

WHEN I WOKE, I wasn't sure of the time, the day, or even my name. Vibrations of excitement hummed within me, but then reality crashed around me. Tomorrow was Christmas Eve and I'd canceled my party. I'd canceled Christmas. I'd canceled my favorite holiday.

As I rolled over, Elvira groaned and stalked out of the room. Adam came in a few moments later.

"How're you feeling?" he asked.

"Miserable."

He walked over and sat on the bed, handing me my phone. "There was a call, but we didn't answer it. They left a voicemail, though."

I took the device and played the recording.

Hi, I'm looking for Bernadette Peterson. This is Terry from Perfect Presents and Parties downtown. I have your wallet. Unfortunately, since it's the day before Christmas Eve, I can't bring it to you. My store will be open late, and then I need to head home. If

34

you could stop by today, I'll have it here for you. If you can't make it today, I'll be here tomorrow until three. I've got to get home and celebrate with the family Again, it's Terry from

Perfect Presents and Parties.

"That's great news!" Adam said.

Finally. Something good had happened to me. At least I could cross the DMV off my to-do list. "I wonder where he found it?"

Adam shrugged. "If that man did steal it, he probably dumped it after cleaning it out and getting your address."

"I'm going to head down there," I said.

"Let me come with you."

"Are you up for that?"

"Sure. I'll even wear a baseball cap so you aren't embarrassed by my snazzy new haircut."

I snickered despite my depression. "Let me get ready."

Ten minutes later, I had run a brush through my hair and changed out of my sweatpants, into my jeans. After pulling on my boots, I was ready to go.

"Gunner and I changed the locks on your house," Adam said. "You now have some deadbolts that Superman would have a hard time destroying."

"That was sweet," I replied, giving him a quick kiss on the cheek. "Thank you."

"Wait! Wait!" Ruby yelled as we walked toward the back door. "I want to go!"

Of course. "Sure, Ruby. Come on."

"Let's stop and get Ned, too. He'll love being out and around."

"You make him sound like a dog," I muttered.

"All men are to a certain extent," Ruby whispered as we followed Adam out the door. "Trust me on that one."

Once in the car, I drove to Adam's to fetch his ghost. The

three of us entered the condo and Ruby yelled, "Ned! Hey, Ned! Do you want to go?"

Ned appeared. I'd spent so much time with him, the bloody shirt no longer fazed me.

"Where're you headed to?"

"Downtown. We're going to look at Christmas lights," Ruby replied. "And you get to ride in the car!"

While alive, Ned had never traveled in a vehicle. While dead, he liked to play chicken in the road with them.

"All right," he said. "I suppose I'd like to join you."

Interestingly enough, Ned couldn't leave his house without my presence—the same as Ruby. Somehow, I'd become a ghost 'pied piper' after being hit by lightning all those months ago.

As we drove, Adam found a radio station playing Christmas carols and Ruby sang along at full volume. I quickly turned it off, finding the music—and my grandmother—only made my mood worse.

"Why did you do that?" Adam asked.

"Yeah," Ruby chimed in. "That's just wrong, Bernie. Just because your mood resembles the poop in a punchbowl doesn't mean you have to make things miserable for the rest of us."

"I just don't want to listen to Christmas music," I grumbled. "Besides, we're almost there."

We found a parking spot off the beaten path. Swarms of people hustled about looking for their last-minute gifts. A chill hung in the air and I wondered if snow was in the forecast until I saw a thermometer outside one of the stores—fifty degrees. Well, it was chilly for Arizona, anyway.

My attitude didn't improve as we weaved our way through the throngs. Just yesterday, I had relished in the crowd, the Christmas music, and the decorations. Today, I found it all annoying as heck. When a man bumped into me,

I elbowed him in the ribs and glared at him despite his apologies and wishes of a Merry Christmas.

Ned and Ruby trailed behind us chatting away about the decorations while people passed right through them. Linking my arm with Adam's, I sighed and leaned my head against his shoulder. "I wish I could find a way out of this funk," I said. "I hate feeling like this."

"You can," Adam said. "Allow the Christmas spirit to seep into your bones."

"It sounds like an infectious disease," I said, chuckling.

"In a way it is... a good one, though. One that should be spread throughout the world."

We stopped at a few window displays and I appreciated not being in a rush. Since Thanksgiving, I'd been going a hundred miles per hour, putting together my party and decorating.

The store Boots and Bags carried custom leather goods. I admired one of their purses in the window and debated mentioning to Adam how much I liked it in case he needed to pick up a last-minute gift, but then I remembered I wasn't celebrating Christmas.

As I glanced up, I caught a reflection in the window of a man passing by behind me.

The very guy who had stolen my wallet!

Anger swelled within me as I turned around and reached out, grabbing his arm. "Hey! You took my wallet!"

His brow furrowed as he pulled out of my grasp. "Excuse me?"

"You took my wallet yesterday!" I yelled. "Then you broke into my house!"

"Get him, Bernie!" Ruby yelled. "Give him a quick kick and make him sing soprano so the copper can arrest him!"

"What's this all about?" Ned asked. "This man stole from Miss Bernie?"

37

As I tugged at the perpetrator's coat again, I wished for the hundredth time Ned would quit with the formalities. The ghost always addressed me as Miss Bernie, and it irritated me to no end when my mood was good. I wanted to kick *him* in the nether regions, but that would be a waste of effort since my foot would slice right through him. Instead, I focused my wrath on my thief.

People began paying attention and stopped to watch. Some pulled out their phones and filmed. I didn't care. My fury boiled.

"You must have me mistaken for someone else," my robber said. "If you'd like to talk about it, we can go inside the store."

He pointed to Boots n' Bags and I shook my head. "The cops are going to arrest you. I've got one right here! Are you out here looking for more innocent victims?"

"Ma'am, I—"

"You're a sorry sack of a human being for ruining Christmas, you slimy jerk!"

Adam placed his hand on my shoulder. "Bernie, stop!" he whispered harshly. "Please calm down for a minute and listen to me."

"Don't tell me to calm down!" I shouted. "This guy—"

"Is a cop," Adam muttered under his breath. "Please remember you're being filmed."

Slowly, I released the thief's jacket and gazed around at the crowd that had formed. I loved my phone. I appreciated the efficiency. Yet, as I stared at all the cameras filming me, I desperately wished the technology had never been invented.

"I'm so glad I made a fool out of myself before FaceTwit and Insta-Toc—or whatever they're called—came around," Ruby said with a heartfelt sigh. "At least back then we could laugh and move on. Now, it's preserved for all eternity on someone's device."

"Let's walk this way," Adam said, placing his arm around my shoulder and turning me away from the crowd. I stared down at the pavement as he led me away, my cheeks flaming with embarrassment.

When we rounded the building and ended up in a parking lot, I glanced up to find the man I'd just accused of robbery following us, along with a few people still filming on their phones.

"All right," Adam said, placing himself between me and the looky-loos. "The show's over. Merry Christmas, and go along with your day, please." After they left, he turned to me. "Bernie, this is Max. He works for the Sheriff's office with me and was put on foot patrol for the holiday shopping season to help prevent thefts and pickpocketing. Max, this is my girlfriend, Bernie. I'm sorry about all of this."

"Why aren't you wearing a uniform?" I asked.

"I'm trying to blend in," he replied with a shrug. "Why did you think I stole your wallet?"

I sighed and explained the happenings of the previous day. "You were the one constant during the afternoon. I actually thought you were following me, and then when we bumped into each other, that's when I was sure you grabbed my wallet."

"And I followed you home and stole all your gifts when you left the house?"

I nodded.

"Nope. Sorry. Not me," Max said, smiling. "I don't even recall seeing you yesterday."

How fitting. He'd been on my radar, but he hadn't even noticed my existence. My embarrassment seemed to have no end.

"She received a phone call that a store owner had picked up her wallet," Adam said. "We're heading that way. Again, I'm sorry about this, Max."

I swallowed back tears of humiliation. I'd acted like such a fool. Grabbing a cop, screaming like a banshee and accusing him of stealing from me while at least a half-dozen people filmed... it didn't get much worse. Well, I supposed I could've been naked, but thankfully not.

Max smiled again and waved. "No worries, Adam. Have a good one, and Merry Christmas."

As he walked back to the stream of shoppers, I wanted the ground to open and swallow me whole.

"Let's go get your wallet," Adam said.

Following him quietly, I was mortified by the scene I'd made and a sick realization that curled my stomach.

I knew who must have stolen my presents. I just didn't understand why.

CHAPTER 6

As I walked into Perfect Presents and Parties, I scowled at all the people lined up waiting to checkout.

"It would be rude for me to cut in line," I said. Adam nodded in agreement.

Ruby, on the other hand, believed it may be a good thing. "You're already all over Face-Tok or whatever it's called for accusing a cop of stealing your wallet. Might as well make it a home run and anger all these people, too. Remember, there's no such thing as bad press!"

Ignoring her and silently disagreeing, I stepped to the back of the line and patiently waited. Ruby and Ned discussed the tables of gifts surrounding us.

"What in tarnation is that thing?" he asked. I glanced behind me and found them huddled over a nose hair trimming kit.

"Men in particular get a few stragglers out their nose and this helps them keep the strays in line," Ruby explained.

"That's ridiculous," Ned scoffed. "We didn't worry about such things in my time."

"Yeah, I figured as much. Were you aware some men actually shave around their stick and berries as well?"

"Stick and berries? What exactly is that?"

I groaned and tried to tune out the conversation.

"What's wrong?" Adam asked. "Are you okay?"

"I'm trying not to listen to the ghosts' conversation," I whispered. "Ruby's trying to educate Ned on some men's choice of hygiene."

"There probably wasn't a lot of that around during his era," Adam replied. "In any form."

"Well, I'll be darned!" Ned shouted. "What kind of nonsense is that?"

"At least they're getting along," I muttered. Sometimes they fought like two siblings.

The line moved slowly until finally, I stepped up to the cash register.

"What can I do for you?" the man asked with a jolly grin as he glanced at my empty hands. Short and round, he wore a red Santa cap and a red shirt and could've passed for one of Santa's elves. The Christmas spirit was in full swing within his heart.

"I'm Bernadette Peterson," I said. "Someone phoned me and said you had my wallet."

With a snap of his fingers, he replied, "Oh! Yes! That was me! I'm the owner, Terry. Hang on just a second. I set it in the safe in back."

The woman behind me groaned and I shot her a glare, but kept my mouth shut. I didn't need any more confrontation for the day.

"Here you go," the man said a few moments later. He opened it up and glanced at my driver's license. "Yep, that's you."

As he slid it across the counter with a chuckle, Adam asked, "Can I ask where you found it?"

"Right here! She left it on the counter after checking out. I tried to find her when I realized it, but there were so many people gathered outside, I couldn't see her."

"Thank you," I murmured. Every single dollar was still wedged in there along with my credit cards. "How did you get my number?"

"Good thing you had a business card stuffed in the side pocket," he replied with a wink. "When my brother and his wife come to visit, I'm going to suggest they stay at your place. I looked up the reviews and they're really good. She fancies herself a psychic, so she'll be into the hauntings people mentioned." He leaned forward as if he were about to share the biggest secret I'd ever heard. "She drives me a little crazy."

Great. The annoying psychic would be staying with me. "I look forward to meeting them," I replied, forcing a smile.

"I can't wait to haunt them!" Ruby squealed. Ruby and I had a rule: she couldn't haunt any of my guests without my permission. She really never followed the directive, but if this woman ever checked in, she could do whatever she wanted to her. Considering Ruby's ghostly abilities were so limited, the haunting wouldn't consist of anything very noticeable. But as a self-proclaimed psychic, Terry's sister-in-law would most likely revel in Ruby's feeble attempts.

"Thanks for calling me about this," I said, stuffing the wallet into my purse. "I appreciate it."

"Can you move along?" the woman behind me asked. "We still have a big line back here and I've got other places to be."

Her Christmas spirit had obviously gone down in a heap of flames, just like mine, and I held my tongue.

I thanked the owner again and we walked out the door.

"At least we've got the wallet mystery solved," Adam said. "Now on to the gifts."

"Oh, I know who took them now." Glancing to my left, in

perfect kismet timing, Henry, my handyman, walked toward us, his arms loaded with bags. I pulled Adam to the right about ten feet. "Let's stay here just for a minute."

"What are we doing?" Adam asked.

"We're watching my thief and gathering evidence."

Henry strolled into Perfect Presents and Parties without noticing us. Ruby and Ned continued to chat while I stared at the man through the window.

After waiting in line, he got up to the counter and unloaded all my gifts from the store bag he carried, handing over the receipts. The owner yakked with him for a moment as he processed the refund, then handed over the cash to Henry.

"Henry stole my gifts," I whispered to Adam. "Did you see him get the money?"

"Are you sure those are yours, or is this another incident where you may be jumping to conclusions?"

Touché. I seemed to have done exactly that a lot lately. I shook my head. "No. He noticed the presents on the couch. We actually talked about them. He also knew when I left. Then he picked the lock on the back door and stole them. Look—the owner is holding the pizza socks I bought. And there's the Public Restroom Survival Kit."

"Those are some great gag-gifts," Adam replied. "I'm impressed with your choices."

"Thanks."

"Was anything else missing from the house?"

I shook my head. "Not that I noticed."

"Why do you think he did it?"

"I have no idea," I replied, shrugging. "Let's go find out."

I followed Henry, my heart aching with betrayal. Dozens of times over the years he'd been in my house fixing things for me. I thought I could trust him, that we had a sort of friendship and mutual respect.

How wrong I'd been.

Just as he was about to enter another store where I'd purchased some items, I hurried behind him and tapped him on the shoulder. His face paled and his eyes widened when our gazes met.

"B-Bernie," he stuttered. "Hi!"

"I know what you did, Henry," I said. My voice sounded tired and weak. I didn't have the energy to be angry any longer.

"What? W-what do you mean?"

"You stole the gifts for my party. I just watched you return them and get cash back."

"Sorry, Bernie. I don't know what you're talking about. I—"

"Please don't make this any worse by lying," I said.

He smiled, but guilt shone in his eyes. "I'm not lying."

"Henry, I know what I saw." Pointing to Adam over my shoulder, I said, "I believe I've introduced you to my boyfriend, Adam, who's a sheriff's deputy."

"Yeah, we've met."

"You want to tell us what's going on, buddy?" Adam asked. "Why you're stealing from Bernie?"

Tears welled in the man's eyes and he couldn't meet Adam's hard gaze. "I don't know what you're talking about."

"Maybe we need to go to the station and discuss it," Adam growled. "Would that be better?"

I didn't think Henry would have stolen from me unless absolutely necessary. He never had before. "It's okay, Adam," I said, placing my hand on his forearm. "We don't need to do that. In fact, I'd like to buy you a cup of coffee, Henry. Then, I'd like to hear why you took my presents."

Finally, his shoulders sagged and a couple of tears tracked down his cheeks. "I'm so sorry, Bernie," he whispered. "I had no choice."

"Come tell me about it," I replied. "Canyon Coffee is just a block away. They've got great scones."

"Well, I never saw this one coming," Ruby said, trailing behind us with Ned. "Henry? Of all the people, I never would've expected that. Always watch out for the quiet ones, Ned."

"Why's that?" he asked.

"Because the quiet ones are the most trouble."

"I tend to be fairly quiet, Ruby. I don't feel I'm much trouble."

"Ned, you were a dang bank robber who took a bullet to the chest!" Ruby scoffed. "If that's not trouble with a capital T, I don't know what is!"

Once inside Canyon Coffee, I spied a table in the back corner and hustled through the crowd to claim it while Adam spoke with Henry, then got in line. He didn't need to take my order; we'd frequented the store often enough for him to have memorized exactly what I wanted.

Henry sat down next to me and placed the rest of my purchases on the floor between us. We waited in silence except for the ghosts arguing about what tasted better: chocolate or cherry pastries. Personally, I loved both and wouldn't turn either away, but chocolate had my vote.

When Adam returned with our coffee and scones, I took a long sip of my vanilla latte, then met Henry's gaze. "What's going on?" I asked.

He sighed and sat back in his chair. "Business has been slow," he said. "There's a new guy in town who has rates I can't meet. I'm not sure how he works for so cheap, but he's been draining my business the past few months."

I nodded, following where the story was headed.

"As you know, I've got four kids, Bernie. And... and I don't have enough money to give them a proper Christmas. Heck, I don't have enough money to give them *any* Christmas. The oldest was on the trampoline last month and broke his arm. My wife, Judy... well, she's got cancer. She's got a fifty-fifty chance of making it. The medical bills are piling up."

"I wasn't aware Judy was sick," I said, now fully comprehending the depth of his predicament. Judy being ill was worrying enough. Add on the cost of getting her well, and the stress Henry was under—this could drown anyone. I'd been in the hospital after being forcefully given an overdose of flunitrazepam, a drug given to insomniacs and also utilized as a date rape drug. The bills were ridiculous.

"When I saw all your presents and the decorations in your house, I wanted to be able to give my kids something. Anything. So yes, I took your presents. I felt awful about it, but I also didn't want to have to explain to my kids that there is no such thing as Santa. I didn't want them to wake up to nothing on Christmas Day. If Judy... if Judy isn't going to make it, I didn't want her last Christmas to be one where the kids found out Santa isn't real. She loves this time of year, and I want it to be happy for her. She's been under such a cloud with the cancer treatments. Watching the kids open presents just warms her heart."

I still couldn't find it within myself to be upset. In fact, just the opposite. I wanted to help Henry. "I don't want any of that either," I said, pointing at the presents on the floor between us. "Take the rest of the gifts you have and return them. Use the money to get those kids some presents."

Adam smiled as Henry's eyes widened. "I... I don't know what to say."

"'Thank you' would be a good start," Ruby muttered.

"Just don't steal from anyone else, okay?" Adam grumbled. "You're lucky Bernie doesn't want to press charges. You could be in jail for Christmas."

"I won't," Henry said, standing and grabbing the bags. "I can't... I can't tell you what this means to me, Bernie. I'm a proud man and I've never done anything like this before. I'm disgusted by the levels I've sunk to in order to give my family a Christmas."

"Just go do the best you can, Henry."

"You're a wonderful human being. Thank you."

As he hurried out of the coffee shop, Adam and I finished our drinks. Suddenly, my heart sprouted wings and I grinned. It seemed my funk had disappeared. "I feel good for what I did."

Adam grabbed my hand. "It's nice to see a smile instead of the scowl you've been wearing since yesterday."

"I was pretty miserable," I replied. "But now, the tree, the gifts, the dinner... it all doesn't seem to matter."

"That's not what Christmas is about," Ruby chimed in. "The Christmas spirit has touched your heart again because you did something nice for someone."

I glanced at the two ghosts standing over my shoulder. "You're right."

"And, you can do even more," Ruby replied, smiling.

"Like what?"

"Don't worry," Ruby said, rubbing her hands together. "Let's pretend I'm the ghost of Christmas future, and I have a plan."

CHAPTER 7

Christmas Eve

IN THE PAST, when Ruby mentioned a plan, it always meant trouble for me. However, this time, she had concocted an idea I could really support. My heart felt as if it would burst right open with joy.

"Okay, are we ready?" Adam asked.

My friends had gathered in my living room, all of them agreeing to participate in Ruby's scheme.

Gunner had put dibs on becoming Santa. We'd found a suit to rent, even though it was about four sizes too big for his fit frame. We'd tied pillows around his midriff, dyed his black beard white and I'd dug up an old pair of dress up glasses from Ruby's chests in the attic. His girlfriend Jezebel had opted to be Mrs. Santa. Thankfully we were able to find a red and white suit for her and once again, Ruby's collection of old clothing and wigs came in handy. Jezebel looked great with gray hair.

Jack, Darla, Adam and I did our best to come up with elf costumes: our ugly Christmas sweaters we were going to wear to my party and jeans. I did discover some elf hats at Perfect Presents and Parties while out shopping earlier in the day.

Darla had pulled together a meal: turkey, gravy, mashed potatoes, and all the fixings. It sat out in her car packed in a warmer. The back of my vehicle was stuffed with presents and my fingers were bandaged with papercuts from all the wrapping.

"I think we're set to go," I said. "Gifts, food, and the Christmas spirit is in full swing."

"Let's head out!" Ruby yelled. "Woohoo!"

We piled into our respective cars, Adam and I riding with the ghosts in my SUV.

As we drove across town, we sang along to the Christmas songs playing on the radio. *Deck the Halls. Jingle Bell Rock. Santa Claus is Coming to Town.* By the time we reached our destination, my Christmas spirit was at a fever pitch.

I pulled out the bags of Christmas gifts from the back end of my car and brought them up to the front door of the small, two-story home. No wreath. No lights. A small Christmas tree had been set up in the window, its white bulbs blinking on and off. Being aware of what the family was facing inside, it seemed downright depressing.

As I stood on the step, I glanced behind me at my crew. Excitement crackled in the air around us. When I'd shared Henry's story and Ruby's plan, they'd all jumped on board, ready to pitch in.

I rang the doorbell and held my breath while we waited. Yes, I was excited, but also nervous. What if Henry's family didn't want us to spread our Christmas cheer? Yet, something inside me told me I was doing the right thing, that our visit was desperately needed.

A small, rail-thin bald woman opened the door, her gaunt brow furrowed in confusion. "Can I help you?"

I'd met Henry's wife, Judy, once about a year ago and I barely recognized her. I cleared my throat. "We're here…"

To do what? Give the kids a nice Christmas? Feed the family? Give them a good memory of the holiday in case she died?

"What's going on?" Henry asked, coming to the door. His eyes widened in shock when he saw me. "Bernie, what are you doing?"

"Let's go in," Ruby said, marching past me and the owners of the house. "Come on, Ned. Let the living work things out while you and I explore as far as our leashes allow."

"Merry Christmas, Henry," I said.

"Ho! Ho! Ho!" Gunner yelled, stepping up next to me. "There're four children on my good list living here and I'm here to deliver their presents!"

"Is that Santa?" a child's voice called from inside. "Is Santa here?!"

Squeals of delight filtered outside along with the patter of little feet hurrying toward the door.

"And I'm Mrs. Santa!" Jezebel said cheerfully. "It's lovely to be out with the big guy and seeing all the kiddos!"

Two girls and two boys burst outside and stared up at Gunner with wide eyes and open mouths. All under the age of eight, their surprised little cherub faces confirmed my friends and I were doing the right thing.

"He's so *big*," one of the younger one said.

Jezebel bent over and whispered not-so-subtly, "That's because he eats too many cookies!"

As the kids grabbed Gunner's hands and dragged him inside with Jezebel trailing behind, Darla introduced herself, "I'm Santa's chef. Have you and your family eaten tonight?"

Judy shook her head as tears tracked down her cheeks. "I'm… I'm so tired. I don't have the energy to cook. We were about to throw in a frozen pizza."

"That's my specialty," Henry muttered. "I'm not good for much else in the kitchen."

"It's great," Judy said. "It's all we need."

"Well, as Santa's chef, I've whipped up a turkey dinner with all the fixings for you," Darla said, taking Judy's hands in hers. "May I bring it in?"

Judy glanced at me and back to Darla. "Why are you doing this?"

"Because we'd heard through the grapevine that this family was in need," I said. "We wanted to help give you a wonderful Christmas."

Judy turned to her husband. "Did you have something to do with this?"

He shook his head. "If you're asking if I planned this, the answer is no."

I wouldn't go into the facts. Henry had stolen from me to give his family a decent Christmas. He'd made it clear they were overwhelmed with bills and worry and I wanted to make it better.

"Come in," Judy said, shrugging. "A home-cooked meal sounds wonderful, and the kids are too excited for me to send away Santa. Excuse the mess. Like I said, I've been tired."

After Darla and Jack fetched dinner from her car, we entered the modest home. The only sign of Christmas besides the small tree in the window were stockings hanging from the fireplace mantel. Gunner had sat in a chair by the living room window and Jezebel stood behind him. The kids had gathered at his feet as Jezebel read *T'was the Night Before Christmas*.

Adam and Jack helped Darla and me get dinner ready. There wasn't a table large enough for us all to sit at, so we decided to place the food out buffet-style and have everyone self-serve. Ned and Ruby stood at the halfway point between the kitchen and living room, watching us all.

"Ned, this was one of the best ideas I've ever had," Ruby said, obviously very satisfied with herself. "Those kids are happier than pigs in mud."

"I agree. This is a very kind thing for everyone to do. Even the mom seems to be enjoying herself. I'm glad I'm here to witness this."

Peeking around the corner, I found Judy sitting on the couch with Henry, her head resting on his shoulder. Both smiled as they observed the kids listening to the story.

Darla tapped my shoulder and motioned me back into the kitchen. "I know I run a restaurant and I'm a clean freak, but this kitchen is pretty dirty," she whispered. "I used the bathroom, and there's dirty laundry overflowing in the basket. This family needs more help than one meal and us in costumes."

For the first time, I took a good look around. The small kitchen had bits of food on the floor and little handprints on the refrigerator and cupboards. I imagined with four small children, it was tough keeping things clean.

I considered running down the hall and throwing in a load of laundry, but it seemed like I was invading their personal space. I'd already pushed in on the family. "Let's clean after dinner while we do the dishes and the kids are opening their presents," I whispered. "I'll talk to Henry and see if they'll be okay with us coming in once a week to help out."

A few moments later, Darla called, "Dinner!"

Adam and I helped the kids pick out what they wanted to eat and got them settled at the table. Judy claimed everything looked delicious, but she'd only be able to eat a bit of mashed potatoes because her stomach was so sensitive from her treatment.

We all gathered in the living room, plates in hand. Henry walked over to the old stereo and found a radio station playing Christmas music.

"I didn't know Santa liked gravy!" one of the children shouted as Gunner stuffed a huge spoonful of mashed potatoes and gravy into his mouth.

"Yes!" Jezebel replied. "Besides cookies, mashed potatoes and gravy are his favorite!"

I snickered and continued shoveling turkey in my mouth. Gunner and Jezebel worked hard to maintain their physiques, and that included a good diet, if one didn't count their love of beer. I bet he hadn't touched mashed potatoes since last year's holidays.

"When can we open presents, Santa?" one of the children asked.

"Soon!" Gunner replied. "After we finish eating. Make sure to clean your plate so you have lots of energy to play with your new toys!"

After dinner, Darla and I cleaned the kitchen while the kids opened their gifts. I peeked around the corner every now and then to see if they liked our choices, and I was thrilled when they screamed and yelled about the pizza socks while sliding them over their tiny feet.

Once we had cleaned up, Santa announced his departure.

"We've got a lot of presents to deliver tonight," he said, hugging each of the children. "We've got to get on our way."

As the kids waved goodbye and asked why Santa was getting into a Ford F150, Adam and Jack explained that the reindeer were hungry and eating some hay at a farmer's field outside of town. The farmer had loaned Santa the truck to come see them. I appreciated their creativity and ability to think on their feet.

"Wait until I tell my friends that Santa and Mrs. Santa ate dinner with us!" the oldest one yelled.

As they gathered around the tree again to study their gifts, Darla, Jack, Adam and I packed up the car and wrapped the leftovers, leaving them for Henry and his family.

"I'm not sure what to say, Bernie," Henry whispered when he caught me alone on the stoop. "I never imagined I'd hear from you again about work, and then you did this. I was horrible to you. Why?"

Laying my hand on his forearm, I said, "I'll be honest, Henry. When you took those gifts, it put me in a foul mood. Well, that and the fact that I thought someone had stolen my wallet and my cat ruined my Christmas tree. But then I realized your actions weren't malicious, but a cry for help." I skipped the part about my ghost coming up with the plan we'd just executed. "And when I told my friends, we all agreed this family needed a little love."

"It's the nicest thing anyone has ever done for me," Henry said, stuffing his hands into his front jeans' pockets. "I was so worried thinking how I'd give the kids a proper Christmas… Thank you."

I embraced my handyman and hoped the Christmas spirit bursting from my heart would somehow envelop him as well. "We want to help more," I said. "Let us come in to clean and do some laundry every week."

Henry stepped away and shook his head. "I can't do that."

"You're busy trying to keep food on your table and Judy needs to rest. Let us help you out."

"I can't pay you."

"That's good because I don't want to be paid."

"It doesn't feel right."

As we bartered and finally came up with an arrangement that was acceptable to both of us, Jack, Darla, and Adam filed out of the house.

"Are we set to go?" Jack asked.

I nodded and explained that Henry would do some odd

jobs around the house and at Darla's diner while she and I came in and cleaned and kept up with the laundry.

"That sounds like a perfect compromise," Adam said.

"I appreciate you all," Henry replied. "Thank you again."

As I turned, I found Ruby and Ned staring at us, grinning like two Cheshire cats. I didn't acknowledge them because Henry had had enough surprises for one night.

"Well, I'd say that was a big success!" Ruby said as we pulled away from the curb and waved at the family standing outside.

"Agreed," I said, sighing. "A perfect Christmas."

"And there weren't any dead bodies!" Adam said.

"With any luck, it'll stay that way," I replied. Although considering my recent history, I had my doubts.

But one could hope.

IF YOU'RE ready for more Bernie and Ruby - and another murder! - you'll want to check out the next book in the series: The Neighbor is Nixed.

When Bernie's new neighbor ends up murdered, Bernie is suspect number one. Download The Neighbor is Nixed.today!

ABOUT THE AUTHOR

Carly Winter is the pen name for a USA Today best-selling and award-winning romance author.

When not writing, she enjoys spending time with her family, reading and enjoying the fantastic Arizona weather (except summer - she doesn't like summer). She does like dogs, wine and chocolate and wishes Christmas happened twice a year.

For more information on her books and to join her author group, please visit: CarlyWinterCozyMysteries.com